Hairy Maclary's SHOWBUSINESS

Lynley Dodd

Gareth Stevens Publishing

A WORLD ALMANAC EDUCATION GROUP COMPANY

In Riverside Hall
on Cabbage Tree Row,
the Cat Club was having
its Annual Show.

There were fat cats
and thin cats,
tabbies and grays,
kick-up-a-din cats
with boisterous ways.
Cooped up in cages,
they practiced their wails
while their owners fussed over
their teeth
and their
tails.

Out in the street,
tied to a tree,
Hairy Maclary
was trying to see.
He struggled and squirmed,
he unraveled the knot,
and dragging his lead,
he was off
at the
trot.

He bounced up the steps,
he pounced through the door,
he pricked up his ears,
and he pranced round the floor;
flapping and flustering,
bothering,
blustering,
leaving behind him
a hiss
and a
roar.

"STOP!"
cried the President,
"COLLAR HIM, QUICK!"
But Hairy Maclary
was slippery slick.

11

He slid under tables,

he jumped over chairs,

15

he skittered through legs,

and he sped down the stairs.

In and out doorways,
through banners and flags,

tangling together
belongings and bags.

Along came Miss Plum
with a big silver cup.
"GOT HIM!" she said
as she snaffled him up.

Preening and purring,
the prizewinners sat
with their rosettes and cups
on the prizewinners' mat . . .

and WHO
won the prize
for the SCRUFFIEST CAT?

Hairy Maclary
from Donaldson's Dairy.

Please visit our web site at: www.garethstevens.com
For a free color catalog describing Gareth Stevens' list of high-quality books and multimedia programs, call 1-800-542-2595 (USA) or 1-800-461-9120 (Canada). Gareth Stevens Publishing's Fax: (414) 332-3567.

Other GOLD STAR FIRST READER Millennium Editions:

A Dragon in a Wagon
Find Me a Tiger
Hairy Maclary from Donaldson's Dairy
Hairy Maclary Scattercat
Hairy Maclary, Sit
Hairy Maclary and Zachary Quack
Hairy Maclary's Bone
Hairy Maclary's Caterwaul Caper
Hairy Maclary's Rumpus at the Vet
Hedgehog Howdedo
Schnitzel von Krumm Forget-Me-Not
Schnitzel von Krumm's Basketwork

Slinky Malinki
Slinky Malinki, Open the Door
The Smallest Turtle
SNIFF-SNUFF-SNAP!
Wake Up, Bear

and also by Lynley Dodd:
The Minister's Cat ABC
Slinky Malinki Catflaps

Library of Congress Cataloging-in-Publication Data

Dodd, Lynley.
    Hairy Maclary's showbusiness / by Lynley Dodd.
        p. cm. — (Gold star first readers)
        Summary: Fur rises and havoc ensues when Hairy Maclary the dog intrudes upon a cat show.
        ISBN 0-8368-2894-1 (lib. bdg.)
        [1. Dogs—Fiction. 2. Cats—Fiction. 3. Stories in rhyme.] I. Title. II. Series.
    PZ8.3.D637Hajh 2001
    [E]—dc21
                                          2001020160

This edition first published in 2001 by
Gareth Stevens Publishing
A World Almanac Education Group Company
330 West Olive Street, Suite 100
Milwaukee, WI 53212 USA

First published in New Zealand by Mallinson Rendel Publishers Ltd. Original © 1991 by Lynley Dodd.

Printed in Mexico

1 2 3 4 5 6 7 8 9 05 04 03 02 01

DATE DUE

OCT 8			
NOV 19			
MAY 9			

DEMCO 38-296